CODE BLOB!

Adapted by **Tina Gallo**

Ready-to-Read

Simon Spotlight

New York   London   Toronto   Sydney   New Delhi

SIMON SPOTLIGHT
An imprint of Simon & Schuster Children's Publishing Division
1230 Avenue of the Americas, New York, New York 10020
This Simon Spotlight edition August 2019
TM & © 2019 Sony Pictures Animation Inc. All Rights Reserved.
For information about special discounts for bulk purchases, please contact
Simon & Schuster Special Sales at 1-866-506-1949 or
business@simonandschuster.com.
Manufactured in the United States of America 0719 LAK
10 9 8 7 6 5 4 3 2 1
ISBN 978-1-5344-4645-8 (hc)
ISBN 978-1-5344-4644-1 (pbk)
ISBN 978-1-5344-4646-5 (eBook)

It was a quiet night at the
Hotel Transylvania spa.
Mavis was napping
when Wendy arrived
with her dad, Mr. Blob.

"But, Dad, I'm not too small
to have big ideas," Wendy said.
Wendy's dad sighed.
He rang the bell on the counter.

"Hi, Mavis," Wendy said.
"I thought you were working
in the gift shop."

"I was," Mavis said.
"I also did some time in room service."
She thought back to a few days ago.
"Eggs three ways!" she announced.

Diane the Chicken was shocked.
Mavis checked the room number
on the bill.
She had the wrong room!

"Now I work here," Mavis said.
She showed Wendy a jar.
It was a jar of face cream
with her dad Dracula's
picture on the label.

Wendy read the label.
She realized her own dad
had made the cream!
"I wish you would let me make
some of my ideas," Wendy told him.
But her dad did not hear her.

"I'm tired of having my ideas ignored and being told I'm too small and cute," Wendy told Mavis.

"Smallness can be a plus!"
Mavis said.

"You are the hero whose
tiny arm unlocks the door
when your dad forgets his key,"
Mavis reminded her.

"I wish he would see it that way,"
Wendy replied.
"Stop wishing and start doing!"
Mavis said.

Mavis walked over to Mr. Blob.
"You look stressed," she told him.
"Follow me!"

Mavis led him to the sauna.
"The sauna gives heat that cannot
be beat!" she said.

Mavis and Wendy left.
Nearby, a zombie was trying
to fix his broken hand.
A witch crashed into him,
and his finger flew off!
It jammed in the keyhole
of the sauna door.
Mr. Blob was locked inside!

Now that her dad was in the sauna,
Wendy brought Mavis to the
blob factory.
"This is where the magic happens,"
Wendy told her.
She showed Mavis the machine
that helped make the blob.

Mavis thought the machine
was awesome.
"Get in!" she told Wendy.

Wendy jumped inside.
The machine slowly started to pull
blob from her body.
"If we are going to prove you can
handle more responsibility,
we will have to move faster than this,"
Mavis said.

"Is there a turbo button?"
Mavis asked.
"Check the manual," Wendy said.
But the instructions were written
in blob language!
"I think it means pull this large
lever," Mavis said.

Just then Wendy felt different.
She looked different too.
She had turned into a giant!

Suddenly, Wendy crashed
through the roof.
Mavis called Hank and Pedro
to help.
"Don't make any sudden
movements until I can figure out
how to make you small again,"
Mavis called to Wendy.

"No way! Here's my chance to be big, big, *big!*" Wendy cheered.

A witch spotted Wendy.

"Code Blob!" she cried.

A group of witches circled Wendy.

They threw magic shrink dust at her.

"It's so tickly!" Wendy giggled.

"Wendy, you need to get small again
before you hurt somebody,"
said Mavis, now a bat.
"No way. Besides, my dad has not
seen me yet!" said Wendy.
"Your dad!" Mavis remembered.

Mavis went back to the sauna. "The heat from the sauna shrunk him and it's all my fault," Mavis said. Mavis tried to open the door, but it was jammed with the zombie finger!

Mavis turned back into a bat.
"Wendy, your dad is in trouble and
needs your help," Mavis said.
Wendy smiled. "He must have heard
that I am big now!" she said.
"No, he needs your *small* Wendy
help!" Mavis said.

"How am I going to get small again?"
Wendy asked.
Just then she spotted Mr. Hydraburg,
the operator of the sauna.

Mr. Hydraburg turned his heads.
The heads breathed fire.
They circled around Wendy,
creating whirls of steam around her.

When the steam disappeared,
Wendy was small again.
She stuck her small finger
in the door to unlock it.

"Daddy! I am here to save you!"
Wendy shouted.
She hopped into the sauna.

"You are so tiny!" Wendy said,
giving him a hug.
"I know how it feels!"